Amelia Earhart

THIS BROAD OCEAN

THE CENTER FOR CARTOON STUDIES PRESENTS

Amelia Earhart

THIS BROAD OCEAN

by Sarah Stewart Taylor
& Ben Towle

with an introduction by Eileen Collins

Disney · HYPERION BOOKS
NEW YORK

First Edition   10 9 8 7 6 5 4 3 2 1
ILS No. G615-7693-2
288 2009
Printed in China
Reinforced binding

Library of Congress Cataloging-in-Publication Data on file.
ISBN 978-1-4231-1337-9

Visit www.hyperionbooksforchildren.com

The Center for Cartoon Studies
P.O. Box 125
White River Junction, Vermont 05001
www.cartoonstudies.org

Introduction

by Eileen Collins

A few weeks before I departed on my first mission into space, I received a very special package. Carol Osborne, an aviation historian, had learned that I was to be the first female pilot of a Space Shuttle and had flown to Houston to deliver one of Amelia Earhart's scarves. Holding it in my hands, I was overwhelmed by the historical significance of this simple, yet lovely, piece of fabric.

I've admired Amelia Earhart for much of my life. As a child, I read about her many accomplishments, such as her solo flight from Hawaii to California and her historic crossing of the Atlantic. When I was a teenager, I took a deeper interest in her as my own desires to see the world took root. I was amazed to discover that not only was Earhart a world-renowned pilot, she was also a published author and

university consultant. And amidst all of that, she found time to design a line of clothing for the active woman! Her passion spoke to my own. I was intrigued by this woman who pursued her goals openly and unapologetically.

Born on July 24, 1897 in Kansas, Amelia spent her childhood in various towns throughout the Midwest. As a young woman, Amelia wasn't quite sure what she wanted to be when she grew up and tried her hand at a number of endeavors. She worked as a nurse's aide, tending to wounded soldiers during World War I. She spent a bit of time at Columbia University in New York City in their premedical program. And she made a living as a social worker in Denison House in Boston, Massachusetts. But Amelia hungered for something more; she craved adventure.

She found what she was searching for on December 28, 1920. On that day, pilot Frank Hawks gave her a ride that would change the course of her life: "By the time I had got two or three hundred feet off the ground," she said, "I knew I had to fly." The following week, Earhart took her first flying lesson. And just six months later, by taking odd jobs, she purchased her first plane, a Kinner Airster that she named *Canary*. How's that for focus and determination!

Over the next several years, Amelia continued developing her aviation skills,

setting records along the way. But she was not able to make a living as a pilot; it simply wasn't something women did at the time. That would change in 1928, after she received a call from book publisher and promoter, George Palmer Putnam, asking if she'd like to be the first female passenger to fly over the Atlantic. Her triumphant voyage (chronicled in her own *20 Hours, 40 Minutes*) brought Amelia a level of attention, acclaim, and money previously unknown to her. And she embraced her new life.

The young pilot was finally able to dedicate herself to flying, but her ambitions stretched far beyond her own career. She became an associate editor at *Cosmopolitan* magazine in order to campaign for greater public acceptance of all women in the field of aviation. Earhart was among the first aviators to promote commercial air travel; she promoted the establishment of separate women's flying records; and she was the first president of the Ninety-Nines, an organization of female pilots providing moral support to fellow female pilots while advancing the cause of women in aviation. Some mistakenly think that Amelia was simply engaged in flying "stunts," but she was, along with other female pilots, crucial to convincing the American public that flying was no longer just for stuntmen and daredevils. Her legacy can be felt every time we go to an airport.

Looking back at my own career, it's obvious the impact Amelia Earhart had on it. As a nineteen-year-old interested in flying, I was apprehensive about approaching a flight instructor; my impression was that they would not want to teach a woman. Later, there were times in the military when I was told that some of my colleagues did not want women in pilot training. But in those moments, I held tight to my dreams, confident in the idea that if I stayed the course, I'd reach my goals. "The most difficult thing is the decision to act; the rest is merely tenacity," Amelia said. "You can do anything you decide to do. You can act to change and control your life. And the procedure, the process is its own reward." And you know what? When I first started taking flying lessons, I was met with respect and energy. In the military, I just kept doing my job, and eventually saw changes in attitudes. Sometimes, taking that first step is the most difficult. And I'm certainly glad I did.

What Earhart achieved in her short lifetime is astounding enough on its own, but to do it in a time when women were expected to be something else...well, I think that is the biggest accomplishment! Amelia opened doors for so many women, including me, in the field of aviation (and beyond). I often think of something that Amelia said: "My ambition is to have this wonderful gift produce practical results for the future of commercial flying and for the women who may want to fly tomorrow's planes." Earhart is remembered for the many records she broke, as well as her mysterious disappearance. But her legacy lives in the hearts of all of the female pilots, adventurers, astronauts, explorers, teachers, mothers, and sisters who dared to fight for change.

I arranged for Amelia's scarf to get manifested on my first flight; NASA made it extremely simple, despite its being a complicated process. Once we addressed all of the rules and regulations, the scarf was carefully folded and vacuum-packed in clear plastic along with the other special items my crew members had arranged to have on board. I took a great deal of comfort and pride knowing that one of Amelia Earhart's possessions was part of my first space mission. Shortly after I returned to Earth, I made sure to get the scarf, along with a whole lot of gratitude, back to Carol Osborne. It is now among Amelia's treasured goods.

Amelia Earhart: This Broad Ocean highlights Amelia's first flight across the Atlantic in 1928. By focusing on one particular episode, creators Sarah Stewart Taylor and Ben Towle are able to offer us a glimpse into this amazing woman's life and hint at the greatness to come: her commitment to her craft and the effect she had on those around her. In Taylor's thoughtful prose and Towle's beautiful art, Amelia's strength, determination, and spirit shine through. I hope you enjoy this book as much as I did.

—E. C.

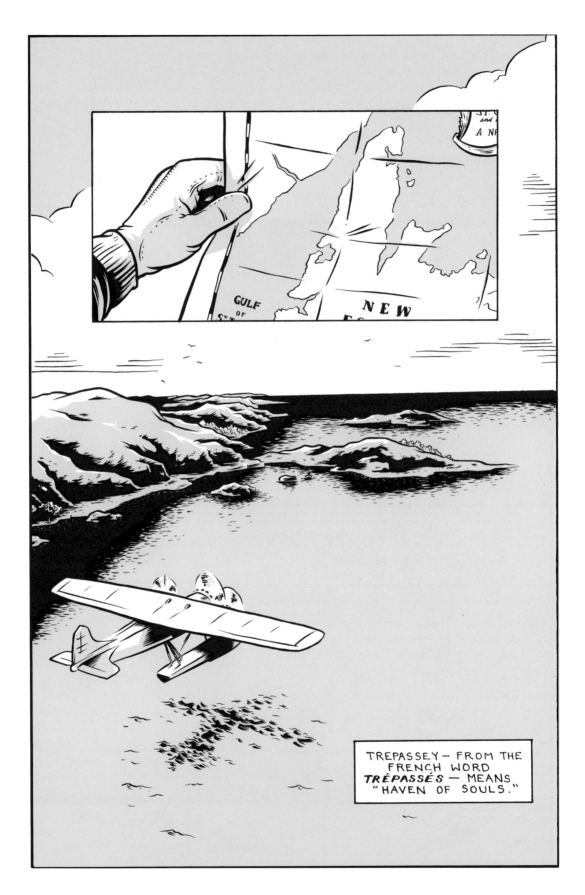

TREPASSEY — FROM THE
FRENCH WORD
TRÉPASSÉS — MEANS
"HAVEN OF SOULS."

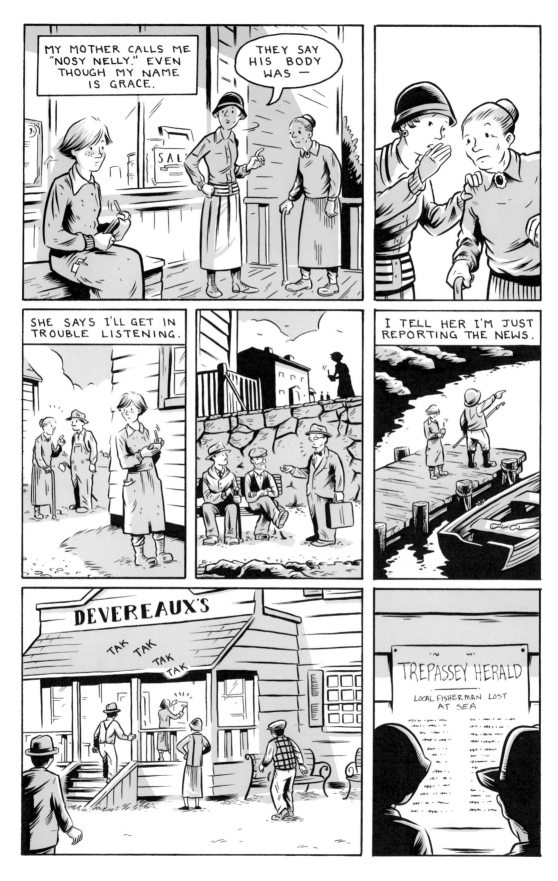

JUNE 4, 1928

THE NUNS ONCE TOLD US A STORY ABOUT A BOY WHO FLEW TOO CLOSE TO THE SUN AND CRASHED INTO THE SEA.

WE KNEW ABOUT THAT KIND OF AMBITION IN TREPASSEY.

IT WASN'T THE FIRST TIME THEY'D COME HERE TO THE END OF THE CONTINENT, LOOKING FOR A HEAD START ACROSS THE NORTH ATLANTIC.

6

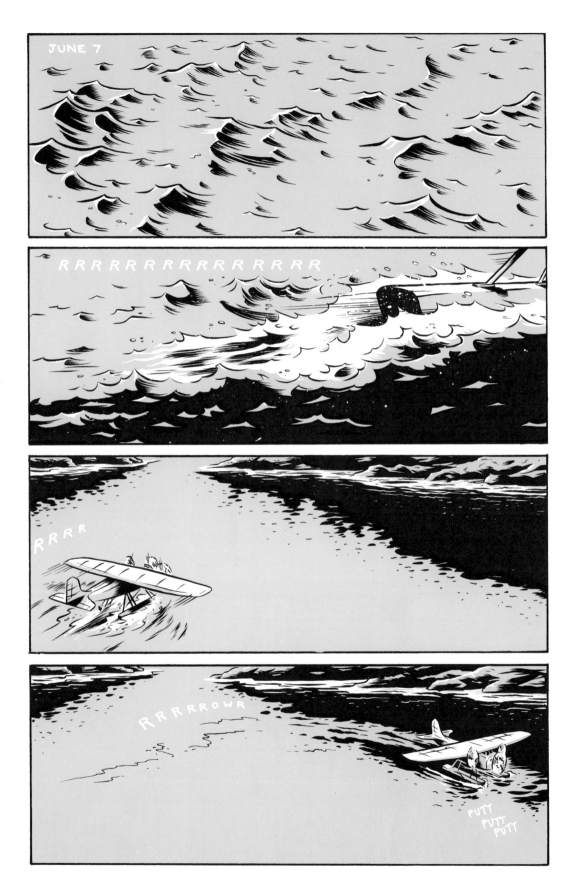

15

SHE FLEW TO HAVANA WITH BILL STULTZ AND SHE SAYS MISS EARHART STOLE HER PILOT.

NOW SHE'S GOT A NEW ONE AND SHE'S CHAMPING AT THE BIT DOWN AT ROOSEVELT FIELD.

AND SHE'S NOT THE ONLY ONE EITHER.

THERE'S A KRAUT LADY, THEA RASCHE, SAYS SHE'S GOING TO FLY FROM LONG ISLAND TO BERLIN IN THE NEXT COUPLE OF DAYS.

LITTLE MISS EARHART HAS HERSELF A RACE.

THEA RASCHE

20

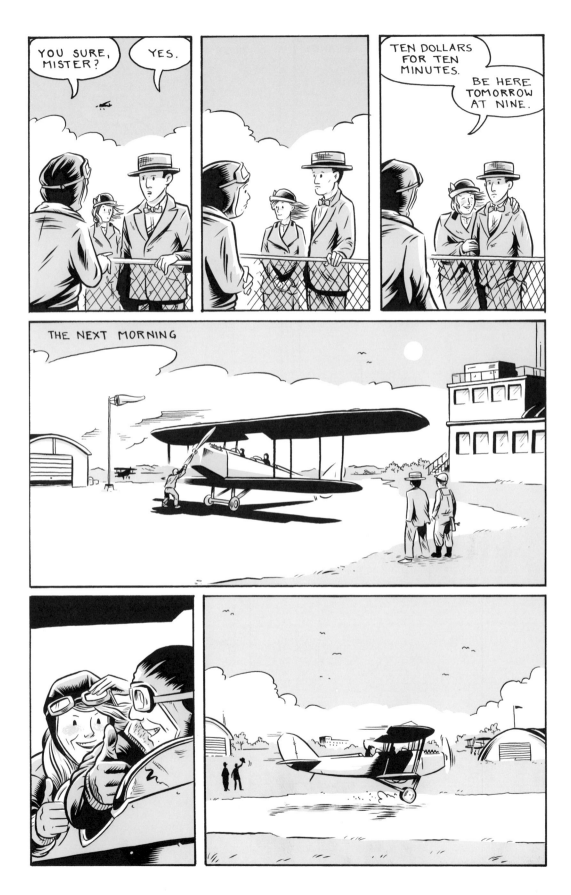

37

BUT WHY DO YOU THINK THE PLANE WILL TAKE OFF THIS TIME?

IT HASN'T TAKEN OFF YET.

YOU *ARE* A REPORTER.

THAT'S A GOOD QUESTION.

WE'LL OFFLOAD SOME MORE FUEL. MAKE THE PLANE LIGHTER.

WE CAN GET DOWN TO 700 GALLONS FAIRLY SAFELY. THAT'S WHAT WE NEED TO MAKE IT ACROSS.

I'M BEGINNING TO THINK IT'S NOW OR NEVER.

BECAUSE OF MABEL BOLL?

BECAUSE OF MABEL BOLL.

BECAUSE OF THEA RASCHE.

AND BECAUSE MY GUT IS TELLING ME THAT IF WE DON'T GO TOMORROW, WE WON'T GO AT ALL.

DID YOU GET ALL THAT?

45

AFTER THEY WERE GONE, NONE OF US KNEW WHAT TO DO.

OR, AT LEAST, *I* DIDN'T KNOW WHAT TO DO.

I HAD MY STORY, BUT I DIDN'T HAVE AN ENDING FOR IT.

MOST OF THE REPORTERS STUCK AROUND FOR DAYS, WAITING FOR THE NEXT BOAT TO HALIFAX.

DEVEREAUX'S

I KEPT THINKING ABOUT 700 GALLONS OF PETROL.

THE ABSOLUTE BARE MINIMUM NEEDED TO GET THEM TO IRELAND.

IRELAND

AND ONLY IF EVERYTHING WENT EXACTLY ACCORDING TO PLAN.

THE TREPASSEY HERALD

EARHART LANDS IN WALES!
FIRST WOMAN TO CROSS ATLANTIC

STARTED IN TREPASSEY

By Grace Goodland

Amelia Earhart, the Boston social worker, is the first woman to fly across the Atlantic Ocean. The historic flight started in our town of Trepassey and took her 20 hours and 40 minutes to complete. Many townspeople wondered if Earhart would ever complete the flight, as she was plagued by poor weather and airplane problems. Despite these obstacles, she won the race against her fiercest competitors, the female pilots Thea Rasche and Mabel Boll, who

were also trying to cross the Atlantic. Miss Earhart's success is sure to bring fame to our humble town. People around the world now know the name of Trepassey, Newfoundland.

LOCAL FISHERMAN DIES AT SEA

Colin Fogarty, a local man, has been confirmed dead at sea. He leaves behind a wife and six children.

HALIFAX, NOVA SCOTIA, 1937

64

SHE'S NOT JUST IN THE PAPERS, EITHER. SHE'S IN THE NEWSREELS, RIGHT UP THERE WITH KING GEORGE GETTING MARRIED AND THE OPENING OF THAT AMAZING GOLDEN GATE BRIDGE.

BUT MOST OF ALL, SHE'S IN MY HEAD, THE WAY I REMEMBER HER, AS I GO THROUGH THE MOTIONS OF MAKING ENDS MEET.

AMELIA'S FROM A SMALL TOWN, JUST LIKE ME, BUT NOW SHE HAS THE WHOLE SKY TO CALL HOME.

THAT'S WHAT MAKES ME THINK HALIFAX IS JUST A STEP TOWARD SOME OTHER PLACE.

MONTREAL. BOSTON. NEW YORK CITY.

PLACES WHERE THEY ARE READY FOR A GIRL REPORTER.

BUT HOW DO I GET TO ONE OF THOSE PLACES?

WORK HARD. SAVE MONEY.

HOPE.

Amelia Earhart

THIS BROAD OCEAN

Panel Discussions

PAGE 1:
"This Broad Ocean"
"Not much more than a month ago I was on the other shore of the Pacific, looking westward. This evening, I looked eastward over the Pacific. In those fast-moving days which have intervened, the whole width of the world has passed behind us—except this broad ocean. I shall be glad when we have the hazards of its navigation behind us."

—Amelia Earhart in Lae, New Guinea, on June 30, 1937, two days before she and her navigator, Fred Noonan, disappeared over the Pacific Ocean en route to Howland Island. Earhart was attempting to become the first person to circumnavigate the globe along the equator.

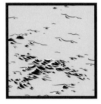

PAGE 2: *Trepassey, Newfoundland*
Trepassey, a small fishing village on the eastern coast of Newfoundland, was a popular spot for pilots trying to fly across the Atlantic because of its location on the Avalon peninsula, North America's closest point to Europe. It had only about six hundred residents in 1928, most of whom made their living as fishermen or subsistence farmers. Despite its popularity as a takeoff point, however, Trepassey's narrow harbor made it less than ideal.

PAGE 6:
Women in Aviation
There were a number of well-known women pilots before Amelia Earhart. In 1908, a Frenchwoman, **THÉRÈSE PELTIER**, was the first woman to fly an airplane solo. The 1920s saw a number of American women take up flying, setting speed records for female pilots, and achieving "firsts." Amelia's first teacher, **NETA SNOOK**, had learned to fly at the Curtiss-Wright School of Aviation, rebuilt a plane she'd purchased after it had been wrecked in an accident, and then taken it up to try it out, even though she'd never flown solo before. **LAURA BROMWELL** was the holder of the women's speed record when she was killed in a plane crash in 1921, the year after Amelia took her first flight. American **RUTH NICHOLS** was an early pioneer for women in aviation. In 1928, she was the copilot on the first nonstop flight from New York to Miami. In 1930, she beat Charles Lindbergh's record for flying cross-country. She and Amelia Earhart, along with other women pilots, founded "The 99s," an organization for women pilots.

PAGE 6: *Career Change*
Though she managed to achieve five hundred hours of solo flight time and to keep up with various flying organizations, Amelia reached

the end of her twenties without distinguishing herself particularly in the world of aviation. She was almost thirty years old and working as a social worker in Boston when she was asked to consider being the first woman to fly the Atlantic.

PAGE 6: *Social Work*

Amelia became a social worker at Denison House in Boston in 1926. Denison House was one of a number of so-called "settlement houses" in American cities, where young, well-educated social workers lived with the urban poor and provided programs to the surrounding poor and immigrant communities.

Social work was an important outlet for intelligent, ambitious young women in the 1920s. College-educated women were not yet entering medicine and the law in large numbers, and social work provided a career path with opportunity for advancement, as well as a high degree of autonomy and independence.

During her time at Denison House, Amelia organized educational programs for residents and the community and even used her flying skills to blanket the city with advertisements for a Denison House benefit. After she returned from her historic 1928 flight across the Atlantic, she lived for a time at Greenwich House, a settlement house in Greenwich Village, in New York.

PAGE 7: *Amelia Earhart*

Amelia Mary Earhart was born on July 24, 1897, in Atchison, Kansas. As a girl, she loved daredevil games and outdoor activities, but it wasn't until she was in her twenties that she took her first ride in an airplane. When she was growing up, Earhart's home life was marked by instability; her father, an alcoholic, had trouble holding down a job. The family moved around the country, and she graduated from high school in Chicago, started junior college at the Ogontz School in Rydal, Pennsylvania, then left school to work as a nurse's aide at a hospital in Toronto during World War I. She started studying pre-med at Columbia University in New York City but dropped out when she realized she wasn't meant to be a doctor.

PAGE 11: *Charles Lindbergh*

Charles Lindbergh, the son of a Swedish immigrant, got his start barnstorming—flying planes in stunt shows across the country—in the early 1920s, and then helped to develop the American airmail system, flying airmail routes in the Midwest. In 1919, a New York hotelier offered $25,000 to the first person to fly nonstop from New York to Paris, and Lindbergh was one of a number of pilots interested in the prize. Three attempts had already failed and ended in death for pilots or crew before Lindbergh took off from Roosevelt Field, on Long Island, on May 20, 1927. Thirty-three-and-a-half hours later, Lindbergh landed his plane, *The Spirit of St. Louis,* at an airfield outside of Paris. He was an instant hero and, along with Amelia Earhart, became the face of American aviation around the world.

His reputation was damaged by his opposition to American involvement in World War II and his support of the anti-Semitic America First movement.

PAGE 16: *Mabel Boll*

Mabel Boll joined the race across the Atlantic with Amelia Earhart. She was one of the most famous—and infamous—American woman fliers. She had no desire to be a pilot, but she very much wanted to be the first woman *passenger* across the Atlantic. Boll had earned the nickname "The Queen of Diamonds," due to her habit of wearing two huge diamond rings. Born into modest circumstances in Buffalo, New York, she became wealthy through marriage and courted publicity, claming that if she made it across the Atlantic, she would greet reporters in a vest made of gold, with buttons made of diamonds.

PAGE 17: *Thea Rasche*

German aviatrix Thea Rasche was the daughter of a wealthy brewery owner and Germany's first and most famous woman pilot. She became known as an aerobatic pilot in the United States and flew in the 1929 first-ever Women's Air Derby.

PAGE 18: *George Palmer Putnam*

George Palmer Putnam was born in 1887 into the famous Putnam publishing family. As a boy, he was fascinated by adventure stories, and shortly after his graduation from Harvard, he left for Oregon, where he became the publisher of the Bend, Oregon *Bulletin* and was elected mayor of the growing town. He and his wife and family returned to New York upon the death of George's older brother. It was now up to him to go to work for the family publishing business, and he began to sign up writers and ghostwriters of adventure stories. Putnam had his own adventure in 1926, when he participated in an expedition to Greenland.

Putnam published Charles Lindbergh's book about his 1927 transatlantic triumph and, ever on the lookout for the next Lindbergh, he heard rumors about Amy Guest's plans and instantly saw the promotional possibilities. When he heard from Guest's lawyer, David Layman, that they were looking for a new woman to make the flight, Putnam started searching. A friend of his asked around in the Boston flying community and found Amelia Earhart. He was immediately taken with the young pilot, and during her time in Trepassey, Amelia corresponded constantly with Putnam. After the record-breaking flight, she moved into the home he shared with his wife, Dorothy, to write her book *20 Hours, 40 Minutes: Our Flight in the* Friendship.

PAGE 30: *Edwin Earhart*

Amelia's father was an intelligent, loving, complicated, and troubled man. A trained lawyer, he worked as a claims agent for the railroad during Amelia's childhood, though he found it difficult to hold on to a job, and the family moved often. A frustrated inventor, he once traveled to Washington, D.C., to register a patent for a signal flag holder for a railroad train, only to find that someone had already patented an identical design. He was considered something of a spendthrift by the family of Amy Earhart, Amelia's mother,

and the marriage was plagued by money problems. More serious was Edwin's alcoholism, and the couple separated many times during Amelia's childhood and young adulthood before divorcing. Amelia never talked about her father's alcoholism and remained loyal to him until his death.

PAGE 33: *First Flight*

Airplanes became a part of Earhart's life after the fateful flight at Long Beach in 1920. Amelia started taking flight lessons from Anita "Neta" Snook, one of the first women pilots, and received her own pilot's license in 1923, the sixteenth woman in the world to do so.

PAGE 36: *"A rich lady"*

Amy Phipps Guest, the adventuresome (she was a fearless big-game hunter and equestrian) daughter of a wealthy Pittsburgh family and the wife of British politician the Honorable Frederick E. Guest, also wanted to be the first woman to travel across the Atlantic by airplane. The news that flamboyant entertainer Mabel Boll (who, like Amy Guest, was not a pilot) was contemplating a trip prompted her to secure a plane and plan her own attempt, but her eldest son found out about it and, along with other family members, prevented her from going, on the grounds that it was too dangerous. Guest wanted to be sure, however, that the woman who made history by crossing the Atlantic would represent the female sex in a good light. Rather than Mabel Boll, she wanted someone educated, genteel, and an accomplished pilot in her own right. Her family lawyer, David Layman, along with publisher and promoter George Palmer Putnam, started searching for such a woman. Through a contact in the Boston flying world, they found a young social worker named Amelia Earhart.

PAGE 37: *"Why does a man ride a horse?"*

In the spring of 1928, Amelia was called for an interview at the office of Amy Phipps Guest's lawyer,

David Layman. Among other things, she learned that her pilot, Wilmer Stultz, and mechanic, Lou Gordon, would be well compensated for their contributions to the transatlantic flight, while her only reward would be gaining recognition as the first woman to cross the Atlantic by air.

After discussing the details of the flight, Layman asked her, "Why do you want to fly the Atlantic?"

"Why does a man ride a horse?" she replied.

"Because he wants to, I guess," Layman answered.

Amelia said, "Well, then," and they both laughed.

The interview convinced Layman that she was the right person for the job, and she was hired.

PAGE 38: *Marriage*

During a period of financial hardship, the Earhart family, living in Los Angeles, took in boarders in order to make ends meet. One of these boarders was Tufts graduate and engineer Sam Chapman, to whom Amelia became engaged in 1924. They never married, however, despite Sam's enthusiasm, and she broke things off after her historic 1928 flight.

At some point during the aftermath of the flight, Amelia fell in love with her promoter and manager, George Palmer Putnam, but she showed the same reluctance to marry. Putnam, divorced in 1929, fared better than Chapman and was able to talk her into it. On the night before their 1931 wedding, Amelia wrote a letter to George in which she said, "You must know again my reluctance to marry, my feeling that I shatter thereby chances in work which means so much to me. . . . In our life together I shall not hold you to any medieval code of faithfulness to me, nor shall I consider myself bound to you similarly. . . ."

Throughout their marriage, George and Amelia shared a love of travel and hiking, and he continued to act as her promoter and publisher.

PAGE 42: *Bill Stultz*

Wilmer "Bill" Stultz was a Pennsylvanian who'd been trained to fly in the U.S. Navy before becoming a commercial and test pilot. He was paid $20,000 to fly Amelia across the Atlantic. During the weeks of waiting in Trepassey, Amelia Earhart became increasingly concerned about Stultz's drinking. He was frequently drunk, and she later told George Putnam that she had seriously considered asking that he be replaced.

Once Earhart, Stultz, and Gordon were airborne, Earhart found a bottle of whiskey that Stultz had hidden in the plane, though she reported that he didn't touch it during the flight.

In the summer of 1929, a year after their historic journey, Bill Stultz was killed in an accident at Roosevelt Field on Long Island, New York. He had taken two passengers up for a demonstration of airplane acrobatics, but the plane crashed, killing all three of them. Though evidence suggested that the crash may have been caused by one of the passengers jamming his feet under the plane's rudder bar, an autopsy showed that Stultz was intoxicated at the time of the crash.

PAGE 59: *The 99s and the Women's Air Derby*

Earhart had been interested in starting a flying organization for women since before her 1928 flight, and she used her newfound fame to recruit members and secure cash prizes for women pilots.

The 1929 Women's Air Derby brought together forty of the most accomplished women aviators. The derby was organized as part of that year's National Air Races and Aeronautical Exposition and featured an $8,000 jackpot to be shared among the first three finishers. It was meant to showcase women's achievements as well as to prove the safety of the brand-new commercial flying industry. Following a derby rule that "no male person will be allowed to ride in this derby race," the women flew solo cross-country in short "hops," stopping in specified towns each day. One participant died when her parachute failed to open, and there were a number of crash landings, but the derby attracted significant attention and showed the country that women were brave and capable fliers. Amelia Earhart came in third.

In 1930, at the very first meeting of the Ninety-Nines—the name came from the number of women who were charter members—Amelia Earhart was elected president. Today, the Ninety-Nines is an international organization of women pilots with over five thousand members.

PAGE 68: *Disappearance* Amelia Earhart and her navigator, Bill Noonan, disappeared on July 2, 1937, over the Pacific Ocean. They had left on their history-making circumnavigation of the globe a month before, on June 1, 1937, after an aborted attempt earlier that year. After about 22,000 miles and stops in Puerto Rico, Venezuela, Dutch Guiana, Brazil, Senegal, French West Africa, Sudan, Pakistan, Calcutta, Burma, Singapore, Netherlands West Indies, and Australia, Earhart and Noonan landed her plane *Electra* in Lae, New Guinea, on June 29, 1937.

On July 2, 1937, they took off for Howland Island, a U.S. territory in the Pacific Ocean. There is evidence that Earhart's plane was experiencing radio problems. As they approached what they thought was Howland Island, they radioed their position to a U.S. Coast Guard cutter. But because of the radio problems, they weren't able to receive transmissions from the ship. The ship lost contact with the *Electra*, and all attempts to radio the plane were unsuccessful. The plane never landed on Howland Island. A huge search effort in the area of Howland Island for the plane and its pilot and navigator was also unsuccessful, as were subsequent search efforts financed by George P. Putnam.

Though there are many theories about the disappearance, most biographers and experts believe that Earhart and Noonan either went down over the Pacific or crashed on Gardner Island (now called Nikumaroro Island), relatively close to Howland. Recent expeditions have found suggestive artifacts on Gardner Island, including an aluminum panel from a plane like the *Electra* and a shoe heel similar to one on shoes Earhart wore in photographs from the flight.

Amelia Earhart was declared dead on January 5, 1939.

Bibliography & Suggested Reading

Butler, Sue and Lubben, Kristen. *Amelia Earhart: Image and Icon*. New York: Steidl/International Center of Photography, 2007.

Butler, Susan. *East to the Dawn: The Life of Amelia Earhart*. Reading, MA: Addison-Wesley, 1997

Earhart, Amelia. *20 Hours, 40 Minutes: Our Flight in the* Friendship. Putnam, 1928. Washington, D.C.: National Geographic edition, 2003.

———. *The Fun of It*. Chicago: Academy Chicago Publishers, 1932 (1977 edition).

Goldstein, Donald M. and Dillon, Katherine V. *Amelia: A Life of the Aviation Legend*. Washington, D.C.: Brassey's, 1997.

Lovell, Mary. *The Sound of Wings: The Life of Amelia Earhart*. New York: St. Martin's Press, 1989.

Rich, Doris L. *Amelia Earhart*. Washington, D.C.: Smithsonian Institution Press, 1989.

Credits

SARAH STEWART TAYLOR is the Agatha Award-nominated author of the Sweeney St. George mystery series, which follows the exploits of an art historian who specializes in funerary imagery. She teaches writing at the Center for Cartoon Studies, and is cofounder of the Writer's Center, a teaching space and drop-in workshop open to the public in White River Junction, Vermont. *Amelia Earhart: This Broad Ocean* is the first graphic novel she has written. She lives in North Hartland, Vermont, with her husband and two sons. Visit her Web site at www.SarahStewartTaylor.com.

BEN TOWLE is an Eisner Award-nominated cartoonist and comics educator whose most recent graphic novel is *Midnight Sun*, which chronicles the fate of an Italian airship expedition to the North Pole in 1928. Aside from *Amelia Earhart: This Broad Ocean*, he is currently hard at work on *Oyster War*, a raucous adventure story set around the Chesapeake Bay at the turn of the twentieth century. Ben lives in Winston-Salem, North Carolina. Learn more at www.benzilla.com.

A graduate from Air Force Undergraduate Pilot Training, EILEEN COLLINS has logged over 6,751 hours in thirty different types of aircraft. Selected by NASA in January 1990, Collins became an astronaut in July 1991 and served as pilot (the first woman to do so) on Space Shuttle STS-63 and later as commander (again, a female first) on STS-93. A veteran of four space flights, she has logged over 872 hours in space.

Series editor JASON LUTES lives and works in Vermont, where he teaches at the Center for Cartoon Studies. His previous books include *Houdini: The Handcuff King* and *Jar of Fools*. He is currently working on on the third volume of *Berlin*, a graphic novel trilogy about the German city during the waning years of the Weimar Republic.

THE CENTER FOR CARTOON STUDIES (CCS), America's premier cartooning school, was founded in 2005 under the leadership of JAMES STURM, who is the creative director of The Center for Cartoon Studies Books. CCS is located in downtown White River Junction, Vermont, in the historic Colodny's Surprise Department Store building. Visit www.cartoonstudies.org.

the CENTER for CARTOON STUDIES

THE CENTER FOR CARTOON STUDIES produces comics, zines, posters, and graphic novels (like this book about Amelia Earhart!). For those interested in making comics themselves one day, The Center for Cartoon Studies is also America's finest cartooning school—offering one- and two-year courses of study, Master of Fine Arts degrees, and summer workshops.

White River Junction, Vermont

VISIT WWW.CARTOONSTUDIES.ORG

Illustration this page: Kevin Huizenga